words & pictures

CORRINNE AVERISS   ISABELLE FOLLATH

JOY

Fern loved Nanna.
She loved her butterfly cakes,
her mantelpiece mice
and her cat, Snowball.

Most of all, she loved her smile.

But recently, Nanna had stopped
baking cakes, the mice were dusty
and Snowball was more like a ball of fuzz.

Worst of all,
Nanna hardly ever smiled.

"What's wrong with Nanna?" Fern asked her mum.
"I don't know", Mum replied. "It's like the joy
has gone out of her life."
"What's joy?" asked Fern.
"Joy is what makes your heart happy
and your eyes twinkle".

"Like when we all do dancing after dinner?

Or when I get the giggles with Ernie?

Or when I go whooshing down a slide?"
"Yes! A lovely big **whooosh!**" said Mum.

Nanna deserved some **whooosh!**, thought Fern.
And if the joy had gone out of Nanna's life
then she would bring it back!
But where would Fern find it?
And how would she carry it to Nanna?
She searched the house for a catching kit.

A tin,

a paper bag,

a saucepan,

a box with no lid,
a lid with no box,
a fishing net...
...and a pointy stick.

Into Fern's catching
bag it all went.

That afternoon, Fern and her mum set off for the park.
There would be plenty of joy there.
No one would mind if she borrowed some for Nanna.

A puppy bounded towards Fern,
its floppy ears flying up and down.
Bounce bounce bounce!
Fern giggled.
She felt the **whooosh!** of joy!

She tried to catch the bounce…

…but the bounce wouldn't go in the box.

On the swing, a baby chuckled each time
her daddy tickled her feet.
Tickle tickle! Chuckle chuckle!
Fern chuckled too. She felt the whooosh! of joy!

She tried to catch the chuckles.
Then she tried to catch the tickles.
But neither the chuckles nor the tickles
would go in the tin.

When Fern reached the duck pond,
a shimmer of sun sparkles rippled
across the water. Fern smiled.

She felt the **whooosh!** of joy.
Nanna would love this, she thought.

She tried to catch the sparkles...
First with her fishing net, then with her paper bag.
Finally, with a scoop from her saucepan.

But the sparkles just disappeared.

Finding joy was easy,
but catching it was hard!
Fern walked home with heavy feet.
She loved Nanna and wanted to
bring joy back into her life.

But her catching bag was empty!

Nanna was snoozing in her chair.
Fern laid her head on her arm.

"What's the matter?" asked Nanna.
"I wanted to catch some joy for you,
but couldn't!" said Fern sadly.

Fern told Nanna about all the things she had seen...

To Fern's surprise, Nanna smiled.
It was the BIGGEST, WIDEST WHOOOSH!
of a smile Fern had ever seen.

"You don't need a tin or a box
or a net to bring me joy," Nanna said.

"You bring me all the joy in
the world just by being you."

The next day, Fern took Nanna to the park...

whooosh!

Together, they found joy
in the most unusual places.

And this time, Fern's catching bag
was full to the brim...

...with Nanna's delicious butterfly cakes!